HAVE YOU SEEN A TREE FOR ME?

Sarah Eccleston

Illustrator

Jenni Goodman

Enzo was born in the Australian bush, high in the twisted branches of a big old gum tree.

He and his mother spent their days munching on gum leaves, sleeping and snuggling.

Enzo had grown into a big strong boy and he thought it was time to find his own tree to call home.

"A tree for me," he said proudly. And with that, he said goodbye to his mum and began his journey.

Enzo walked ...

and walked ...

and found himself travelling through a paddock filled with cattle.

He asked one of the cows, "Have you seen a tree for me?"

The cows were **big** and **scary**. They weren't very friendly ...
they didn't say a word, they just chased poor Enzo!

He ran up a little tree to safety.

"Well," he panted,
"they weren't much help at all!"

Poor Enzo was tired and hungry
so he rested in the little tree.

Enzo tasted one of the leaves. "YUCK!" he said as he spat the leaf out.
"These are not gum leaves, they taste terrible."
Enzo's little tummy grumbled.
"This tree is not for me!" he muttered.

As the sun went down and it began to get dark,
Enzo snuck down the little tree, past the sleeping cows
and out of that scary cow paddock.

He found himself walking along a big black path.

As Enzo walked he could see two bright shining eyes coming straight towards him.

NEXT
15 KM

"Maybe they will know **where a tree for me is?**" he sighed.

As it got closer, the eyes got bigger and brighter.

Enzo jumped out of the way just in time as the big eyes ZOOMED past him.

They were not big eyes at all – they were lights! Lights on a big truck! The black path was a ROAD!

Enzo knew that a road was not a safe place for him at all.

Enzo was tired and hungry. "I need a tree for me!" he cried.

Poor little Enzo was scared and lonely.
He wished he had a friend around. Just then, he saw a face ...

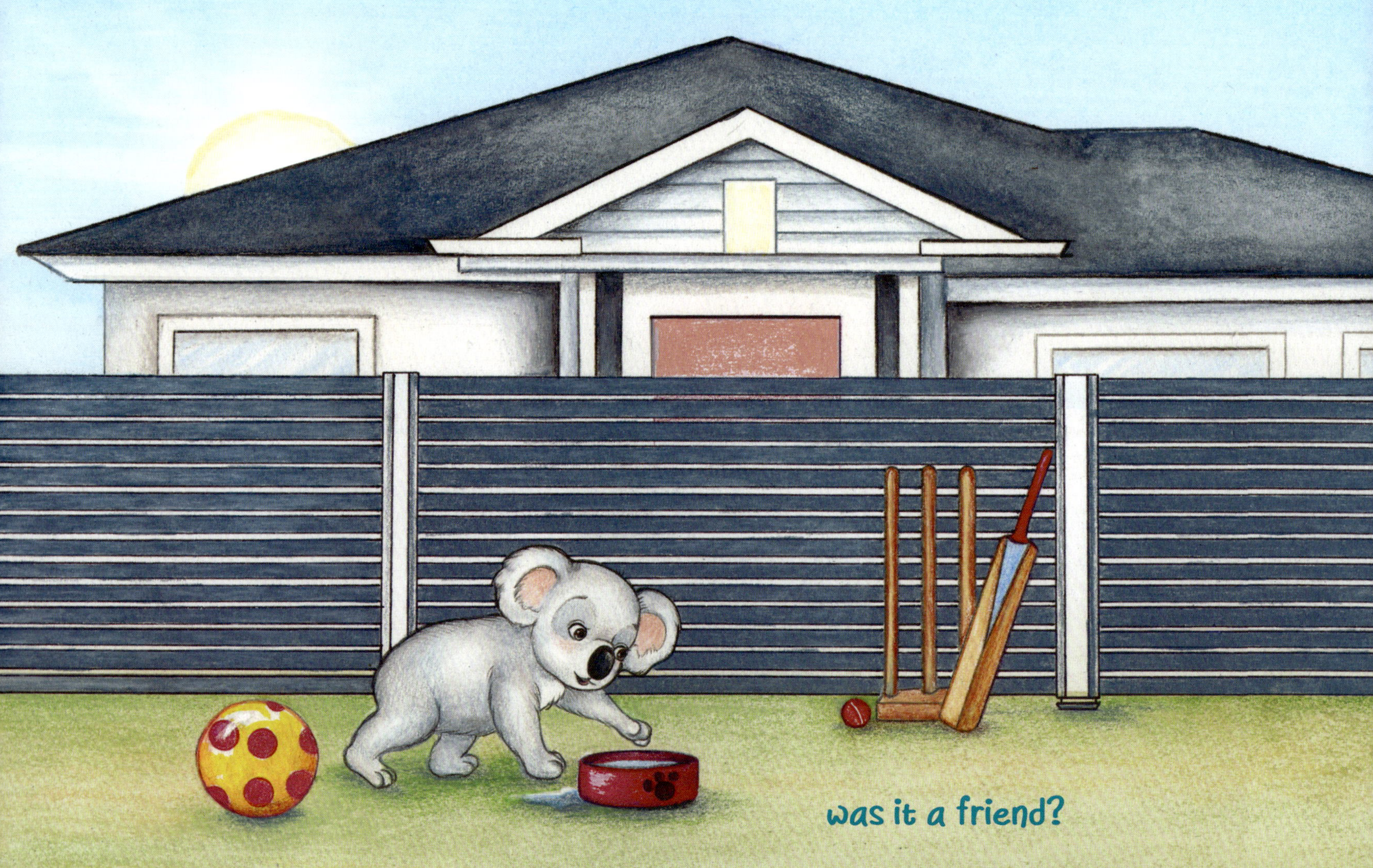

was it a friend?

"Hello, will you be my friend?" Enzo asked.

"WOOF! WOOF! WOOF!"

Enzo was sure a dog wasn't going to be his friend.
So Enzo ran.

He RAN away from the big, loud barking dog.

"WOOF! WOOF! WOOF!"

ZOOM SCREACH ZOOM

He RAN down the road with all the fast cars and trucks.

"Mooo!"

He RAN through the paddock full of big grumpy cows.

"Is this a tree for me?"

He finally found a big tree and climbed straight to the top!

"ENZO?"

It was his mum.

"Oh Mum!" Enzo cried as he jumped into her arms. "I don't think I'm ready to be a big koala yet."

"The world can be a scary place for a little koala," said Enzo's mum as she cuddled him tight.

Back in his mum's tree, Enzo was finally safe and full and sleepy.

"Is there a tree for me, Mum?"

he said as he drifted off to sleep.

"I hope so."

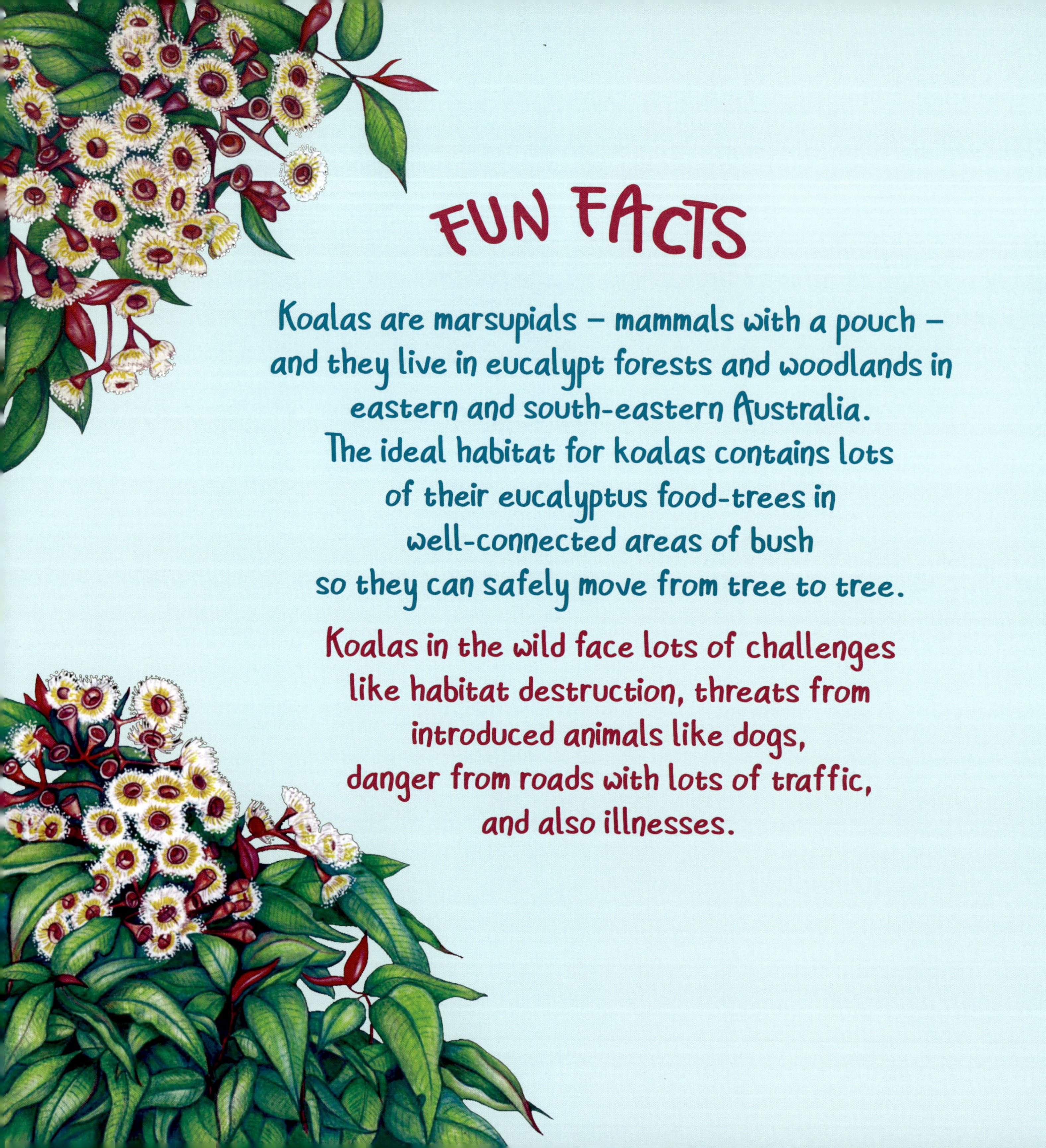

FUN FACTS

Koalas are marsupials – mammals with a pouch – and they live in eucalypt forests and woodlands in eastern and south-eastern Australia.
The ideal habitat for koalas contains lots of their eucalyptus food-trees in well-connected areas of bush so they can safely move from tree to tree.

Koalas in the wild face lots of challenges like habitat destruction, threats from introduced animals like dogs, danger from roads with lots of traffic, and also illnesses.

How can we help koalas like Enzo?

Be a responsible pet owner.
Keep your pets inside at night.

Ask friends and family to drive carefully, especially at dawn and dusk, as koalas are most active at these times.

Protect koala habitat – this could even be your own backyard.

Plant a koala food tree: 'a tree for me'.

This book is dedicated to all of Australia's Koalas, in the wild, in care and in our amazing Zoos and Sanctuaries.

And to my best friends Simon and Jett, love you forever *xxx*

First published in 2020 by New Holland Publishers
Published in paperback in 2022 by New Holland Publishers
Sydney

Level 1, 178 Fox Valley Road, Wahroonga, NSW 2076, Australia

newhollandpublishers.com

A record of this book is held at the National Library of Australia.

ISBN: 9781760791247 hardback

ISBN: 9781760794330 paperback

Managing Director: Fiona Schultz
Project Editor: Liz Hardy
Designer: Yolanda La Gorcé
Production Director: Arlene Gippert

10 9 8 7 6 5 4 3 2

10 9 8 7 6 5 4 3 2

Other Children's Titles:

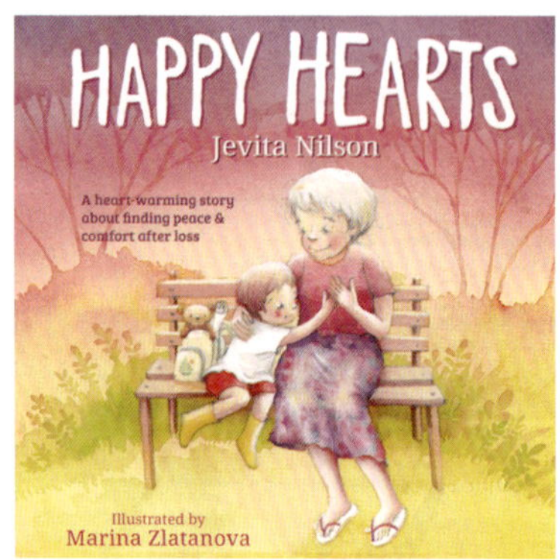

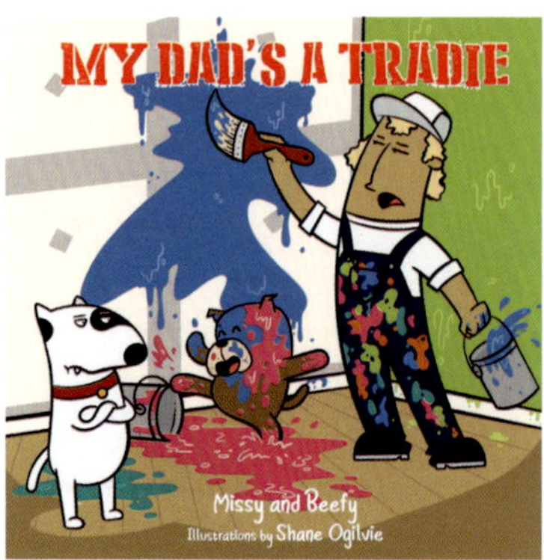

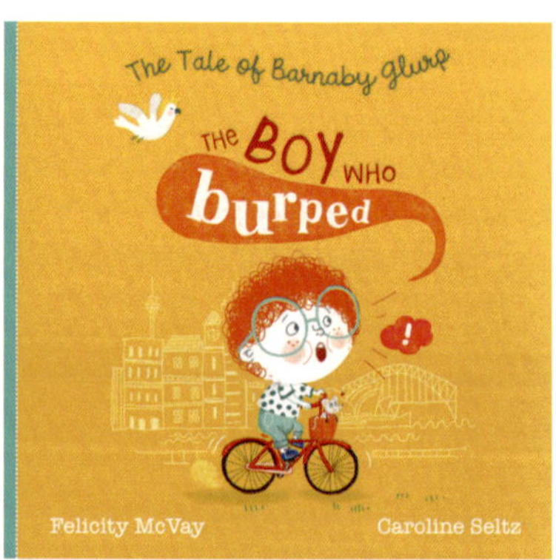